Séance Tea Party

Also by Reimena Yee

The World in Deeper Inspection
The Carpet Merchant of Konstantiniyya

Reimena Yee

Séance Tea Party was conceptualized in a Moleskine notebook, sketched and penciled using Procreate on an iPad Pro, then colored and finished in Photoshop. It was lettered in the author's hand.

Visit us on the Web! RHKidsGraphic.com • @RHKidsGraphic

Educators and librarians, for a variety of teaching tools, visit us at RHTeachersLibrarians.com

Library of Congress Cataloging-in-Publication Data
Names: Yee, Reimena, author, artist.
Title: Séance tea party / Reimena Yee.
Description: First edition. | New York : RH Graphic, [2020] | Audience: Ages 8–12. | Audience: Grades 4–6. | Summary: After watching her circle of friends seemingly fade away, Lora is determined to still have fun on her own, so when a tea party leads Lora to discovering Alexa, the ghost that haunts her house, they soon become best friends.
Identifiers: LCCN 2019043693 | ISBN 978-1-9848-9415-1 (paperback) | ISBN 978-0-593-12532-8 (hardcover) | ISBN 978-1-9848-9416-8 (library binding) | ISBN 978-1-9848-9417-5 (ebook)
Subjects: LCSH: Graphic novels. | CYAC: Graphic novels. | Ghosts—Fiction. | Best friends—Fiction.
Classification: LCC PZ7.7.Y44 Se 2020 | DDC 741.5/973—dc23

Designed by Patrick Crotty

MANUFACTURED IN CHINA
10 9 8 7 6 5 4 3 2 1
First Edition

A comic on every bookshelf.

To every child—and young adult—who is afraid of growing up.

When I was ten, I read fairy tales in secret and would have been ashamed if I had been found doing so. Now that I am fifty, I read them openly. When I became a man, I put away childish things, including the fear of childishness and the desire to be very grown up.

—C. S. Lewis

Captain! Captain!
The ice— it just won't break!
Nonsense, matey.

It's gonna happen.

CRAK
Hooray!
Look alive, crew!
We're free!
Salem

WHEEE!
Chapter 1:
Séance Tea Party
OAKSFIELD CEMETERY

Sup, Lora!
Race ya to class!
Bobby, wait!
See ya later.

ST★RZ
?
Boy
Bar

!
GAMER
SQUAD

AUG 25
SEPT 20
OCT 16

Carol
happy birthday Lo!
Nasrul
it's 2day already?
06:30
Fri, Oct 30
(15) new messages
RIP
Happy Bday
Bobby
haha
Oct 28th
can I borrow your notes?
Yep.
Where are you?

MYSTERIES

Bobby
Fast lyfe
Last online:
Yesterday,
9:13 pm

Sigh

The SUPERNATURAL
Hmm, wowee.
The world is so strange and fancy.
Don't you agree, Lucky?

Whatcha reading?
Ooh, spooky!
Phantasm
Ghosts!
Do you think they are real?
I heard my school was built on top of a grave site...
But that's, like, every school in the country.
Why do ghosts like being in school so much?
BLEH!
If I were a ghost, you know where I'd haunt?
Disneyland.

Bloody Mary
White Lady
Will-o'-wisps
Séances
Hmm, feeling an idea coming...
Snap
Let's hold a séance!
And not just any séance—
a séance tea party!
C'mon!

Ghost Phone
yes
No
ABCDEFGHIJKL
MNOPQRSTUVWX
YZ
HI
GOODBYE
Perfect!

Badazing!
Badazam!
Ghost Phone
YES
NO
ABCDEFGHIJKL
MNOPQRSTUVWX
YZ
HI
GOODBYE
'Lo!
I call upon Merlin and the ghosts of ancient past. Hear!
I've got COOL questions for you.
WOOOOSHHH
William Shakespeare, if you're here, what is the secret to your genius?
Jeng jeng jeng jeng
MAGIC

Of course!
How obvious.
Thanks, mister.
hehe
Another question:
So, my ah-ma burns paper money for my ah-gong sometimes.
I'm curious.
Do y'all actually use money in the ghost world?
MAYBE
Hmm.
Do you like this party?

Huh?
Y E S
Oh, thank you?
My tea parties are legenda—
Whoa.

Eep!
No, no! Don't go away!
I'm a friend.

There you go!
Oh wow! Are you really a ghost?
Discovery TV is gonna get a kick outta this!
What's your name?
Alexa.
Hey! I'm Lora Xi!
How long have you stayed here?
I don't know. A long time, maybe?

WOW! I had no idea our house is haunted. Do you usually show up like this?
No... I mean, I'm a ghost.
People run away from ghosts...
Oh, okay.
Do you have any ghost friends?
No. Just me.
You must be lonely, then...
17:51
Oct 30
That's the afterlife.
That's life too.
HEY! Let's be friends!
Oh?
Sure, if you want.
Really?
I've never heard of anyone being actual friends with a ghost before.
What do you think that would be like?
(Well-)

It'd be a lot like having imaginary friend, right?
I know I had one a few years ago, then one day...
I dunno.
She was gone.
...?
Wanna dance?
Oh.
Okay.
Sure?

Me and my imaginary friend—we used to do everything together.
We climbed trees, played house, and actually...
We used to dance like this too.
Like we were two princesses, waltzing in a ball—

-room...

It's you, isn't it?
nod

EEEEE
Oof!
Oh no!
I'm sorry! I forgot to make myself corporeal.
Haha. No worries. It's cool.
Can I touch you now?
plap

Whee!
I'm so glad you get to be my best friend again!
Aw, me too.

Chapter 2: Halloween
meow meow meow me—
07:30
SLAM
07:30
It's today!
07:31

Here's our little witch!
Happy Halloween.
Any spooky plans with Bobby today?
Nope! He hasn't had time lately.
I'm hanging out with Alexa instead.
Oh, who's she?
The ghost who lives in our house.
We're best friends now.
Cool, cool.
Eh, ah girl, don't you think you're too old to play like this?
You're 12, right?
Shouldn't girls your age be into... I dunno —
Boy bands and fashion?
BLEH!
WHAT lah, you!
Why are you so in a rush for her to grow up?!
PIAK
oi!

Lora, I remember you had an imaginary friend when you were small. Both of you had so much fun!
And the way you used to talk about them...
It was almost like they were real.
Okay, wait, humor me. Do you think this friend might actually be a... ghost, haunting us?
snorts No.
I don't think so.
Do you?
Shrug
Who knows?
There's magic in this world we can't explain.
Haih, as long as this "friend" doesn't disturb us, I don't care.
Oh, I gotta go now.
Bye, honey.
Bye, witchy!
Don't get possessed!

Alexa?
You there?
Yes?
Whew!
Y'know, when I woke up, I wasn't sure if you were real or a dream—
But, well, here you are!
Come look! I brought some stuff.
What is it?

Since you've been a ghost for ages, I thought it'd be fun to show you what all the kids like now.
What's that?
It's a tablet.
Like a smaller TV?
Oh, you know what a TV is!
Well, it's kinda like that, except you can ask this TV to do anything you like.
It's got games, movies, books, the internet...
The internet?
You'll love the internet!
old cartoons
You can find anything you want on it instantly.
All you gotta do is type in your requests in this box here...
And VOILÀ! magic!
WOW!

Hey! I know this! I saw it once in the movies.
Ah, for real? This cartoon is from the seventies!
You gotta tell me what life was like back then!
Was it all in fuzzy color?
Why did everyone speak and dress funny?
I actually... don't remember much from my life.
Really?
I can recall pieces, like my name, and things can be familiar.
But I can't bring up memories on my own.
It's mostly a blur.
Weird.
Yeah, I've no idea why...
How do you see the other stuff in this tablet?
Here, lemme show you.
09:30
Oct 31
Oh! It's Halloween!
Yeah!
It's my favorite holiday!

It's got spooks and candy and all the things I love!
Like trick or treat!
Ohmigosh, Alexa! You gotta join me for trick or treat tonight!
How?
I'm a ghost.
Psh!
We'll make it work.
But what about your, erm... non-ghost friends?
Nah, they aren't coming.
Why?
They are too old for stuff like this.
The cool thing now is to go to the big kids' Halloween parties.
You weren't invited?
... I'm not going.
messages
carol Party at 8!
Carol Hey Lora, u coming?
Lora Got plans. Sorry!!!
Oh...
because you already had one for your birthday, right?

Nah,
I just don't like parties.
Anyway, I wouldn't miss trick or treat for the world, even if it means going out by myself.
And guess what?
I think I know the perfect costume for you.

Isn't this, uh...
A bit on the nose?
Nuh-uh! It's perfect.
Let's go!

Ma, I'm heading out now!
For trick or treat?
Yeah!
Don't come home late. 9 pm max.
Got it!
Whee!

Haha, look at you!
You're a natural!
Well...
I've been practicing a long time.
Boo.
Hehe, nice try! But I'm a witch—
I'm not scared.

Come, my minions!
Let's magic up some sweets!

BWARE
BEWARE OF DOG
RIP
SPOOKY

ding dong
Three, two, one...
TRICK OR TREAT!
Wait...
Sunni!
You live here now?
Hey, Lora!
Haha, yeah, I just moved.
Ohmigawd, it's been like, what, two years?
How you been, gurl?
Pretty okay.
You?
Eh, just life.
New school.
New house.
Who's your ghost pal?
This is Alexa.
She's an old friend.
Aw, cute!
Say, would you like to join my Halloween party?

Oh!
It's a small party. Just me hanging out with some high school buds.
No pressure, though.
Erm... oh gosh, the big kids? I don't know...
Can you give us a sec?
She's your friend, right?
It's gonna be fine.
Besides, this is your chance to see what a real big kids' Halloween party is like!
Sigh.
I know, but...
I'm nervous.
Will you come with me?
Only if you go.
Alrighty!
We're partying.
Awesome!
C'mon in!
Lemme tell my ma that I'm here first.

Hey, gals!
We've got guests!
Everyone, meet Lora and Alexa!
Hey!
Aww, I love your costumes!
AYA
EMILY
OH-EM-GEE, are you a sheet ghost? I LOVE IT!!
HIYA
Way cuter than the trashy costumes they sell in stores.
Ha! You mean like—
Ms. Sexy Sea Cucumber.
Seductive anxiety.
The Male Gaze.
snorts
You nerds.
There are babies in this room now, so you three better behave.
You hear?
Yes, Ms. Prissy.
We'll be on our BEST behavior.
hehe
hehe

So, how did you know Sunni?
Erm...
I was her mentor in Oaksfield Middle.
Then I left for high school, and we lost touch for a while.
'Cause you didn't have a phone back then, right?
But I do now!
Congrats, baby!
I remember when I first got mine...
Hey, Alexa, isn't it stuffy under there?
?
You can take it off if you want.
ERM!!
Sh-she can't!
Huh? Why not?
Eerrr—
I got hives.

OMG!
Holy h— I mean, oh cr— I MEAN—
Oh geez, I'm sorry!
Is that the thing where you get welts all over your skin?
Yeah.
shrug
It's fine. It'll go away. But for now, I'm not comfortable showing myself. Sorry.
Oh, that's smart, wearing that sheet.
It's all cool. If you ever need anything, let us know, okay?
Sure.
NOW!
Where did we stop last?
Boys!
Waitwaitwait—have y'all seen the latest J-Monáe video that just landed 'cause WE NEED TO TALK ABOUT IT AAAHH
Girls!

?
Hey...
What's wrong?

I knew this would happen.
What would?
Sigh.
That I'd be left out.
I mean... look at them.
They are having fun talking...
And I can't keep up.
Why not?
Aren't they friendly?
No!
Yeah, I mean,
just...
Sigh.
It's the same issue with the kids in school too...
They talk about celebs and memes and all kinds of stuff —
But the topics change so fast every day and...
I fall behind.
I stop talking.
Sometimes I wonder if people are pretending to still talk to me so they don't hurt my feelings...

That's why I don't like going to parties.
They remind me of how boring I am...
Lora.
I've only been with you since yesterday.
But I know you're someone with tons of interesting things to say.
You like to read, right?
Yeah, and...?
Talk about that!
But it's all weird stuff!
Like the Bermuda Triangle and Bigfoot and...
It doesn't matter!
I know nothing about that stuff!
But I'd love if you would tell me more!
And I'm sure they will feel the same!

It's not "cool," though...
LORA! Don't let that make you afraid to be who you are.
If they don't jive with that,
SO WHAT?
Your real friends don't love you for how "cool" you are—
They love you.
For you.
CLICK
?
It's the night of nights, when we gather round for one very special event —
GHOST STORY NIGHT
Woot!
Lora, Alexa! Join us!
Yay!
Yeah!

Okay, gang. Here are the rules:
1. Tell us a ghost story.
2. Make it SPOOKY.

We'll move around in a counter clock-wise direction.

So, when I was nine, in my old school, I had to go pee, real bad.

TOILET

The hallway to the toilet was so empty, and so quiet...

And the toilet itself was like that too. No one was in there, and despite it being well-lit, there were dark shadows inside the cubicles...

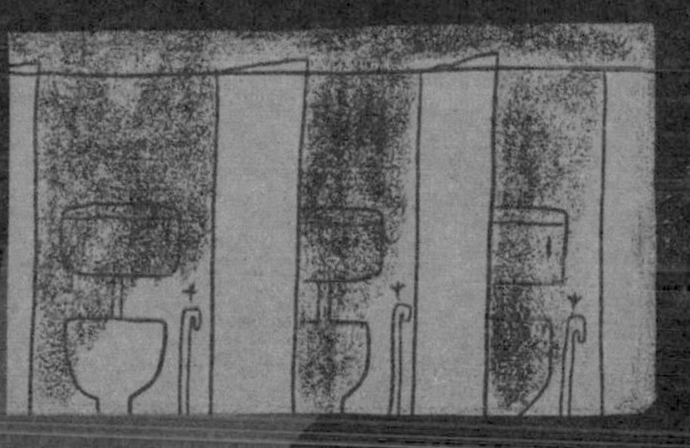

Ohh, nope.

After I was done, I went to wash my hands.

There was this long wall mirror above the sinks.

I looked up—

... and her.
Excuse me? HER? What!
I thought she came in after me. Normal stuff.
Then I looked closer...
... and, gawd, I knew it instantly.
She wasn't anyone I knew in school.
Not anyone alive.
She was standing there staring at me, like —
"Dude, why did you wake me with your flushing?"
At this point, I had given up and just RAN the heck outta there!
aaahhhhh

LORD! You're lucky she wasn't mad!
Right?
Thing is, I'm still not sure she's real.
I mean, no joke, the toilet was super spooky!
Yiiikes!!
Here, your turn now.
Huh?
Er... I... I don't have a ghost story...
Not my own anyway.
But I read in a book—
About this one house in Spain fifty-ish years ago—
where a family first discovered on their concrete kitchen floor...
FACES!
Or, well, images of faces that come and go for no reason over a span of twenty years...

Wait, are those, like, random faces, or...?
Yep!
It's actually a really common phenomenon.
Do you know faces have also materialized—
in water
on toast
on shrouds
and in mirrors?
Ohh, is it like that legend when you say a name three times and a face appears?
Hmm...
What's it called again?
Bloody Mary?
Yeah!
Interesting.

Hmm, my bathroom has a big mirror.
Let's do it!
WHAT?!
You nuts? After YOUR story?
Aya, do you believe in ghosts?
NO.
I mean, I don't know!
Then you've nothing to be afraid of!
Besides, what's the worst that could happen?
Maybe you'll see that sophomore Greg Koh's face in the mirror ~
he he
Urgh, seriously, Sunni! You're gonna get us in real bad trouble someday!
Aw, chill, Aya. We don't live in a horror movie.
Lora, Alexa! C'mon!

I can't go.
They wanna see a ghost, right?
Why?
I'm gonna be that ghost.
WOOOOOOO hehehe
You go on. Tell them I'm sick.
But...
It'll be okay.
Trust me. You'll have fun.
You coming?
See ya.

Alexa's not joining.
She's still queasy from the hives.
Righto.
Make yourself at home! Holler for us if you need to.
Thanks! Have fun!
to-do
UnTrend

Chapter 3: Bloody Mary

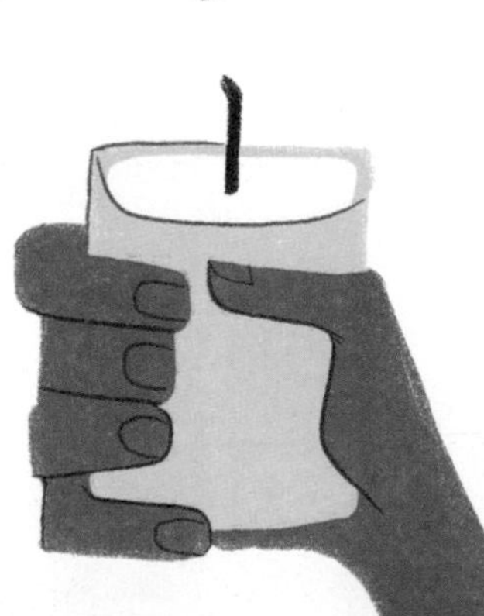

Stand in front of a mirror, look into it,

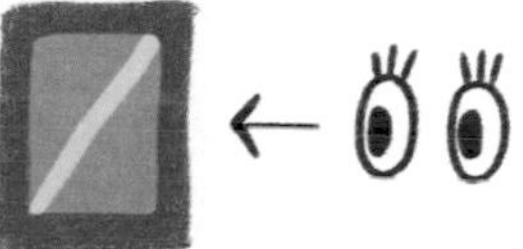

and chant "Bloody Mary" three times.

flit
Thanks for bringing up Bloody Mary.
I was running out of party ideas.
Have you always liked spooky stuff?
Yeah.
Just that I never talked about it with anyone, 'cause it's... weird?
Are you kidding!
I'm into it too, like big-time!
Really?
Yeah!
There's a huge community of spooky geeks online too.
I usually get my content from listening to podcasts.
Huh? Podcasts?

You've no idea what those are?
shakes head
Oh gosh! You're missing out!
You're in for a treat, Lora! Sunni knows the coolest stuff!
SLAM!
Oof! Lemme in!
Hey!
OKIO-DOKIO!
I'm ready!
Lord help me...
Let's. Meet. A GHOST.

All right, door's shut.
Hands together.
Face the mirror.
Ready?
Three, two, one . . .

Bloody Mary.
Bloody Mary.
Bloody Mary!

Haha! Guess it didn't work! Let's goooo!
Wait—

What's this mark?
squeak
squeak

AAAAHH AAAAAAAAAH
AAAHH
Run! Run! Run!
OW!
Geez, your big butt!
Alexa?
hehe

Did you see anything?
You wouldn't believe it —
We saw her! We really saw Bloody Mary!
She was just a face.
A whole face.
Oh wow, really? hehe
What's she like?
Meh, I wasn't really looking.
Oh gosh, I hope we didn't set off some kinda curse.
Lora, sweetie, how are you still so calm?
Err... yeah?

Good news, everyone!
wiki
According to SCIENCE—
wiki page
Dim lights can trigger the mind to hallucinate.
That, plus fear, is what made us see Bloody Mary!
URGH, Em!
Why do you have to be such a nerd?!
kekeke~
But that's why I'm fun at parties.
Well, real or not, I ain't sleeping with the lights off tonight.
Hard agree.
nods
Wait, you're having a sleepover?
Yeah!

Oh no! It's almost nine o'clock.
We have to go now.
Awww.
We liked having you here.♥
Thanks for coming to my party!
We had a blast.
Oh, oh! You should totally join us for the next sleepover!
Oh wow! Really?
Yeah! I just need your number.
Oh, wait, are we trading phone numbers now?
Hey, I want yours too!
Me three!

BOO!
WHOA!
Hehe, I didn't know ghosts can get spooked.
Well, now you know.

Whatcha reading?
Oh.
I picked up a magazine in your friend's room earlier.
I was curious.
Teen Power
Teen Power. Fashion trends for the more stylish you.
Don't miss J-Monáe's... This new meme is taking over...

Ehhh.

You really like using that tablet, huh?
Yeah!
I think it's far out.
It really knows how to find anything.
No regrets going to a big kids' party, hmm?
... Nope.
Sunni
Thanks for making me go.
yawn
And for helping out.

You're the best.

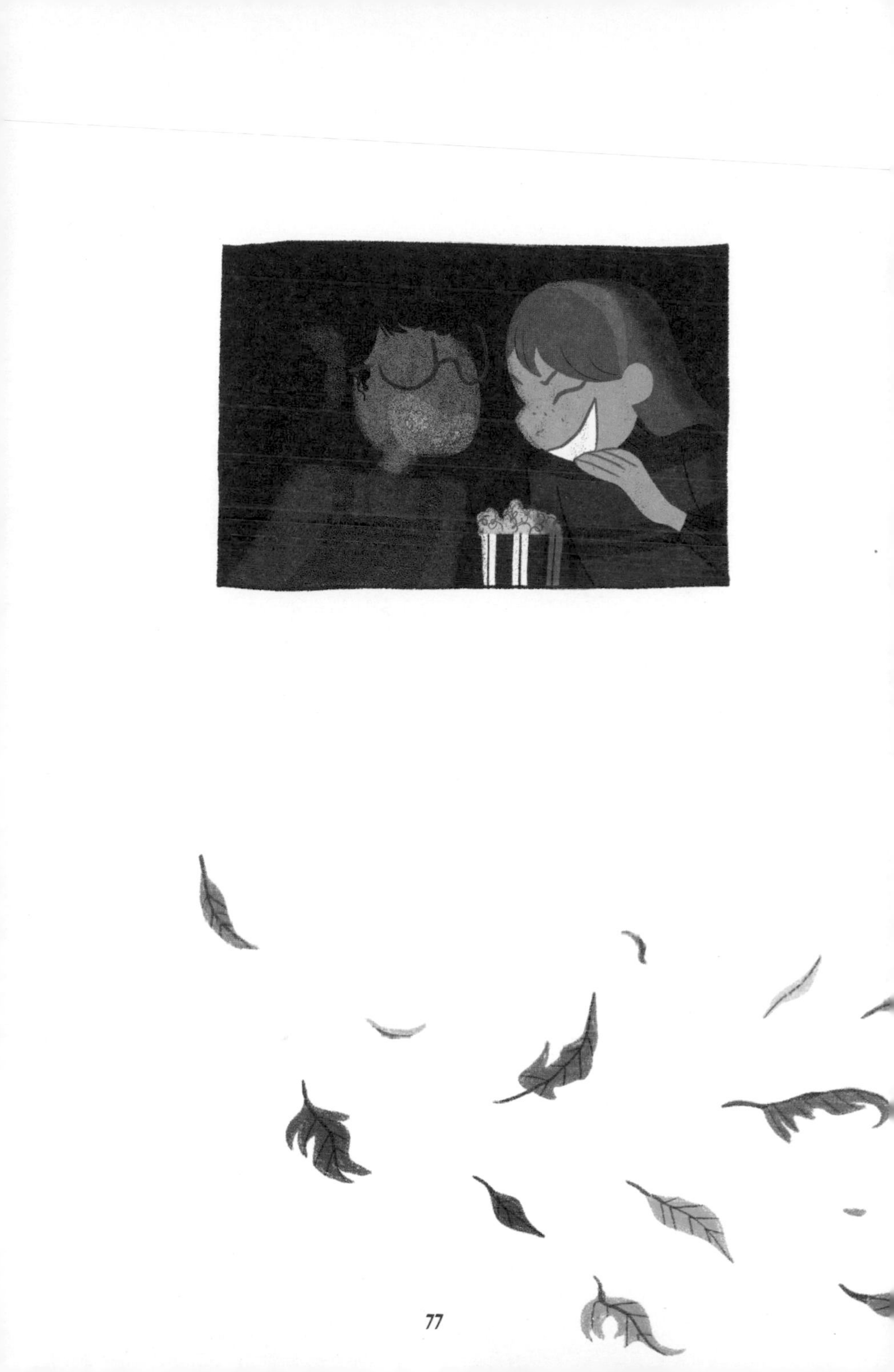

Chapter 4:
Play Pretend

whee!

Do you still remember where this is?
Yes.
We're near the magic Place, right?
We used to play there a lot back then...
All the way up on that hill.
We have quite a bit of a hike ahead.
Oh! Silly! SHOO!
Am not food.

'Kay!
Are we ready?
Let's go!

Oof.
Gimme a sec.
I don't remember the hike up being this brutal.
This place has changed a bit since I was last here.
Yeah.
They paved over most of the dirt path for the new campsite half-way up.
It's all concrete now,
which hurts my feet...
Why don't you use the broom?

Huh?
What for?
Oh, why did you bring it along, then?
Well...
It's 'cause I wanted to be a witch's apprentice today.
I like dressing up as whatever I wanna play as.
It makes it feel more real to me.
Rad! Do you have a story for your apprentice?
Hmm.
Lemme think...
TOK

I'm on an assignment.
The Wizard Council has tasked me to find a magical fruit—
Which only grows from the biggest tree on this hill.
But I'm not in a huge rush.
I'll wander for a while.
C'mon!
Right, left, right, left!

But!
I can't linger for too long.
The Wizard Council wants the fruit real bad!
So I get on my broom...
Then I'll FLY—
—the rest of the w—

Feeling like a real witch now?
Alexa! Are you doing this?! How—?
Hehe~
Hold on.
What is hap—

WOOAAH!!

Oh no! my shoe!
CAUGHT

Woohoo! I'm really flying!
Yeah!
We used to do stuff like this when we played together.
Add some magic, and VOILÀ!
It's an adventure!

Hang tight.

Haha-yeah!

Oh wow.

We're right above the Magic Place. Wanna come down?
Mm-hmm.

ah!
I missed coming here.
You haven't been?
Not really.
You saw how much work it took getting up here.
It wasn't fun going up alone.
So I stopped.
None of your friends wanted to join you?
Did I say something wrong?

No.
No, you didn't.
It's true.
Nobody wants to hang out with me.
Not anymore.
Oh no...
How come?
...
I dunno. Everybody has been drifting away lately.
Nobody wants to play...
Not in the same way they used to.
I remember what it was like being friends with everyone in my entire grade, since our first day in kindergarten. How we all used to talk and be whatever we wanted. The only limit was our imagination.
For a long time, things were simple. We were carefree.

Now all everyone cares about is being grown up.

They want to be part of this big world, caring about who's popular or what's trendy . . .

POP!

They stopped being the kids they used to be.

While I . . . I'm still the same.

I don't know how to be friends with my friends anymore.

So I've just been hanging out with myself lately.
What's keeping you from joining your friends?
Sigh.
It's so silly, but...
It's because I...
I'm scared.

I'm scared of growing up.

I don't want to be a teen yet.

I'm not ready to let go of all the things that make me happy.

I'm scared that...

...once I choose to leave this world behind...

I can never find it again.

Lora,
you never have to choose.

You can be a kid for as long as you like.
It'll be okay,
because I'll be here to keep this magic with you.
We'll have each other, always.

Thank you, Alexa.
I love you.
I love you too.

Chapter 5:
Old Friends

meow meow meow
06:40

You ready?
Whenever you are!
Right!
Three,
two,
one—

OFF

OAKSFIELD MIDDLE
Hmm, this place...
It all feels so familiar.
Maybe you studied here before?
Maybe.
Yeah.
If I did study here, it sure looks fancy now.
Uh-huh.
Oh, hey, you wanna come along with me to class?
... Nah. I'll pass.
I wanna tour the school.
See what's changed.
Cool, okay!

BBRINNNNG
See ya after school!
1976

?
Hey.
Erm...hi?
Who are you?
I'm Alexa...
I'm an imaginary friend.
Oh wow!

Manny!
Come in for class!

LINE ENTRY

Hey.
...Hey.
Happy belated birthday.

Seriously?
Yeah, I . . . gah.
I'm sorry, Lo.
It's not like I forgot.
Just that . . .
There was a lot that went down last weekend.
Was that why you weren't here on Friday?
. . . Yeah.
I'm sorry —
for ignoring your texts, and not being there for your birthday.
You got me a gift, though?
No, Lo.
It's more serious than that.

Sigh.
I fell out with some guys who I thought cared about me...
The things they joke about... I couldn't stand their toxicity anymore.
Real friends don't abandon you after you stop being "cool" to them. We all got to have each other's back, you get me?
And I realized that was what I didn't do for you.
Urgh.
Man, I'm such a jerk.
...
Look.

If you don't want to talk to me anymore, I getchu. We're cool.
I only wanted to let you know I messed up.
I'm sorry.
I hope I'll earn your forgiveness one day.
Hmm, I accept your apology.
Tentatively.
Whew.
Thanks, bro.
You gotta do more than just giving me cat ears, though.
Haha!
Of course, as you wish.

19 81
19 82
19 83
19 73
19 74
19 75
19 76
19 77
19 78
19 80
81
OAKSFIELD MIDDLE
19 76

Alexandra Hudson
Class of 1976
Class of '76?
I knew I was a ghost for a long time...
Diana Rodriguez
but has it really been
almost fifty years?
Jenny Tan
Seamus Brown
They have all grown up now...
My friends...
OAKSFIELD MIDDLE

BRINNNGG
Abuelita!
I climbed the monkey bars today.
Did you? Bueno!
My new friend Alexa helped me – she has flying powers!
Haha!
That is very handy!

You know...
I used to have a friend called Alexa too.
Diana?
WHOA!
rustle

Abuelita...?
Huh.
I must have heard a clumsy squirrel.
My whole world has changed without me...
And I didn't realize...

How was school?
You wouldn't guess who came up to me today!
Bobby!
Oh, you mean, the cat who ignored you?
Haha, yeah, that cat.
Turns out he was having a rough time with his ex-friends.
He apologized for ignoring me. He didn't mean to.
But it's okay now.
So we made up, kinda.

Is he back to being your best friend, then?

No idea.

We lost touch for a while.

Hopefully we'll find that spark again moving forward.

I can't wait.

brake

Are you . . . scared of not being my best friend anymore?

No.
Just . . .
been thinking of how the world has changed.

Alexa!
You'll be my best friend forever!
THAT will never change.
I swear!
Yeah.
I know.

Chapter 6:

Part I: Growing Up

Bobby
Hey bro, wanna hang Fri?
Lora
Totes!
Fri
Lora
Thanks for letting me play Chef Chaos. So fun!
Bobby
IKR. It's wild!
Lora
I wanna play again!

Sunni
did you finish the podcast yet??
what do you think? :)
Lora
I'm only halfway but OMGGG so spooky! I love it!
Emily
RIP @ me. Rly gotta find time to listen to it
Darn it, exams!! FREE ME
Lora
Haha oh yeah, I'm swamped too.

CHILDREN AHEAD

Lora
I know nothing about makeup.
Emily
lol same
I'm curious to see how I'd look with it tho . . .

Sunni
emi, let's!!!!
find out, I mean.
oh you too, Lora!
Aya
MALL TRIP
Hiya
MALL TRIP
Emily

Lora

I've always seen the girls in cartoons wear dark lipstick and really liked it.

But it never occurred to me that I can do that in real life?

I'm so glad it looks good. I feel like I'm more myself on the outside now.

chats!
sunniallday
couple of boba before watching #
lol was it as scary as they said?
chats!
sunniallday
SQUAD! #bffs
love yall <3
chats!
sunniallday
15
it's this lil goblin's bday! love to hate ya!! LOL
wow RUDE

Chats!
dansemacabre
Dad got me a fancy polaroid for Christmas! Thanks di!!
old drawings
after the 25th
PUNK!!
fancy headband
the magic place

Watch it, Bobby.
You don't wanna ruin our poster.

How mad do you think the Student Club would be if I did?
Why don't you find out yourself?
keke
See ya.
TICKET
SPRI
PROM

BRRINNGGG

ideas—

Cafe Rue 15

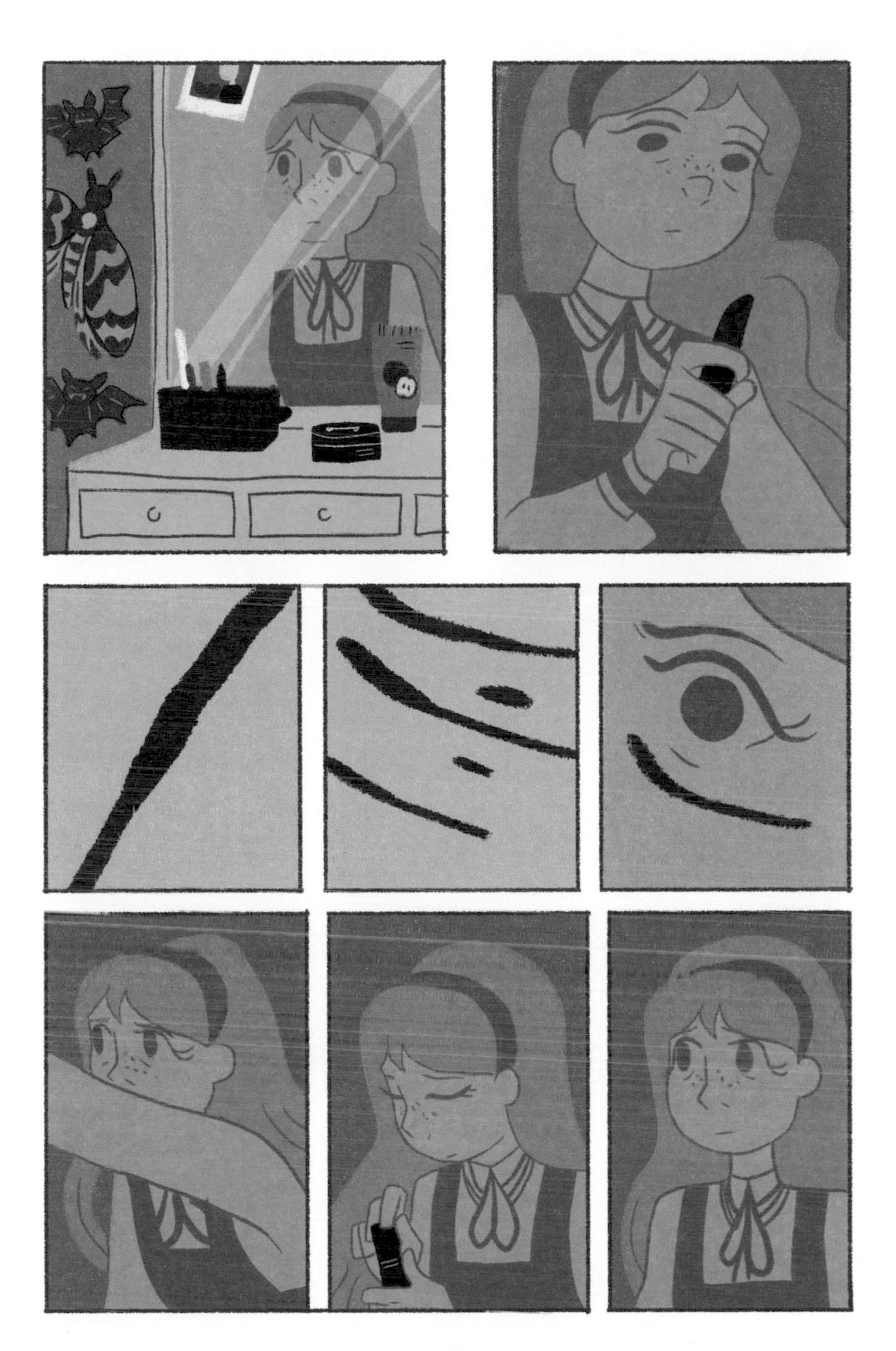

Chapter 6:
Part II : Growing Old

Hey, Allie!
Thanks for waiting!
Aaaah!
I'm going to my first sleepover tonight!
How rad!
Are you sure you don't wanna come?
Sunni and the others miss you.
Haha, not really.
I don't think I can pull off wearing a blanket twice!

Anyway, I have my own plans.
Oh, really!
Yeah. I was thinking...
I want to try exploring the neighborhood on my own.
Now that I'm more confident finding my way around.
Yay!
That sounds awesome!
Maybe you'll stumble on a cool spot...
like a secret catacomb—
...
Uh-oh.

I'M LIVIN' ON THE EEEDGE
WOO!
Eat my dust!
AS IF!
C'mon!
Let's catch up to him!

BRINNNGG
Hehe, why are you so wriggly?
'Cause you're coming to play after school!
HONK
manny!

Abuelita!
Alexa is gonna come visit our house to play!
Is she now?
Hello, Alexa!
I'm happy to have you join us!

Da da da! whooshh
Hehe!
Mijo! Mama is here!
Si!
I'm going home with Mama now.
Are you coming?
No.
But I'll see you in school on Monday.
Okay!
Bye-bye, Alexa!
Bye-bye.

ding

National Writer's Award
presents
Diana Rodriguez
Lifetime Achievement Award

Writer weaves world with magic

Hello there.
Need anything?

Wh-I—erm...
aren't you afraid of me?
Afraid of you?
Haha!
What for?
I'm old—
I've seen many strange things in my life.
Never imagined I'd have a ghost as a houseguest, though.
What's your name?
Alexa.
As in, my grandson's imaginary friend, Alexa?
Yeah, and also...
your old friend from school...
Alexandra Hudson.
SNORT

You're joking?
No, sorry.
Whew. All right.
Bienbienbien.
Dios mío. I'm sorry.
It's a lot to take in.
I know.
You died when we were . . . what? Fourteen?
Was that how old I was?
Yes. It's been some fifty years. . .
Why did you come back?
I never left.
Then how am I able to see you now?
You just do, and. . .
you didn't run away.
Kids don't run from me. They see me as their friend. But with grown-ups. . .
They don't look.

Heh.
I always pride myself on being a child at heart.
Part of my craft.
Speaking of —
I make books for children.
To me, it's important to keep the mind and spirit young. Not just to make good stories —
The Fairies of Faring Forest
Diana Rodriguez
But also to live a good life.

Diana.
Hmm?
What was I like, when I was alive?
You don't remember?
Ah.
How do I begin?

This is the story of a girl, one Alexa Hudson.

She was a sickly child. Her illness made it hard for her to be with other children.

She stared out the window every day, and longed to run and jump and play . . .

. . . just like everyone else.

As she grew, she became well enough to attend school.

For a while, she learned to make friends, to laugh, and to blossom.

Sadly,
it was not to last.

Before her fourteenth birthday,
she fell ill once more.

It caused her so much pain,
she was forced to stay in bed.

Her parents sought help from the best doctors. Her friends tried to restore her joy.

Nothing worked.

And left for a different world, where she would never endure another day of pain and tears...

Or, at least—

Thank you, Diana. I...
I think I get it now.
For a long time, I couldn't remember who I was before I died...
But I must have forgotten on purpose at the start.
If I forget everything — the hurt, the sadness, and all the years I lost...
I can start over and stay a child forever.
That was all I ever wanted.

Chapter 6:
Part III: Growing Out
Cafe with Caroline
Nasrul's 1st championship
To-Do
em ø Math pg50-1
o set up art account??
o meeting with student club @ 3
oh yeah, talk to B about design
800 fans
92 follows
art.soul
dansemacabre
Lora X
BBQ
Art Club
End of Year

← Oaksfield Middle
Cemetery Road →

zziplack

Oaksfield Middle Student Club
invites you to:
The Summer PROM
• food • drinks
• dances • music
• prom royalty
AND MORE
JUNE 1
6PM
The Hall
Grab your tickets at
the counter in the lobby.

Oh!
Before I forget...

Come look.
These are some of the things that were precious to me as a child.
This toy camera, Mr. Bunny Bombom, a few love letters...
Hehe!
Look at how cute we were.
bffs forever

At least you still have your good looks.
Me? Hoho.
I've aged into a wizened, wrinkly crone.
Sigh.
Are you kidding?
You're beautiful.
You're so lucky to be alive—
And to have its gifts marked on every part of you...
Please, Diana.
Keep growing old.

Cherish it.
HAPPY BDAY
bffs forever

Miss Lacy's Vintage Shop
oaksfield

DEAL

. . . I still have NO idea who I'm gonna ask out to prom.
GAAAAHH.
Why is it so hard?
Even Bobby's got a date already!

Check out his date, though.
He's so cute, right?
Okay, lemme show you my options. . .
Wheeee! Indecision— I loovee it!

300!
Picking out clothes is WAY easier.
Should I go all black?
Too goth?
Or floral?
Hmm.
Maybe I should try going all out since this will be my first prom. . .
Then again–
Would it be worth the investment?
It's happening.

It never ends.
Again.
And again.
Year by year—
Living vicariously through other people's childhoods...
As if...
It'll replace the life I lost.
What am I doing?

I am tired —
Of watching everyone move on without me.
When is it my turn?
Look at her.
ding
She's all grown up.
And me?
I need to grow up too.

chapter 7:
Graveyard

Darn!
I keep forgetting.
It's a lovely morning here in Oaksfield!
Enjoy it while you can...
As we'll be battered by a real beast of a thunderstorm this evening.
03
Expect a dreary rush hour, commuters.

And keep your feet dry!
Oh! Good morning, Alexa.
I didn't hear you ring.
...
You don't look happy.
What's wrong?
Diana, I...
I want to go.
Go? To where?

Touch me.
gasps
I can't feel you anymore.
You used to have a presence.
A kind of coldness.
I'm fading. I...
I'm losing my will to stay.
It's... it's nearly time.

That's why.
Is there anything we can do?
No. It's my choice.
I can't keep being a ghost girl forever.
I hope you understand.
Alexa...
Sigh.
If that is your wish,
then I must accept it.
Thank you.
But, please—
Is there anything I can do for you?
Well...
Could you walk with me around Oaksfield—
One last time?

I'M HOOOME!
Haha!
Aren't your folks out? There's nobody here.
Yep, I know.
Sure.
Hey, I'm gonna use your bathroom, then I'm gonna leave.
Okie dokie.
Urgh!

What a day!
I spent most of it sweating over who I was going to ask to prom at the last minute.
I wasn't really feeling any of the choices, so I was like,
Dang! I may as well go solo!
Salem
But then it hit me.
I already know the perfect gal to ask!
It's YOU, Alexa.
Will you go out with me tonight?
Salem

...
Allie.
You there?
...
HELLO?
Yo, who are you shouting at?
EEP!

B-bobby! You're still here?
Urgh, yeah. Sorry.
I just lost my last baby tooth.
LOOK!
Ew, gross.
Yep, gross!
Au revoir, Mr. Tooth!
But seriously, why were you yelling?
Haha!! I dunno! I just like keeping the ghost in my house company!
...
You're weird, you know that?
You used to talk with these characters you'd make up for us to play with.
Haha, those were good times.

Not that I don't believe you!
Ghosts? I don't doubt that spooky stuff! I swear!
em
Oh, dang. I gotta go.
My boyfriend's getting antsy.
See ya at prom tonight, Lo!
Bye, ghost in the house!
slam
Salem

Alexa,
please come out.

Allie?

Alexa!
Alexa!
Where are you?
Please tell me you're up here...
Salem

She's gone.
Did I...
push her
away?

No!
No.
She can't be gone!
She's my best friend!
Salem
She wouldn't leave me like this...

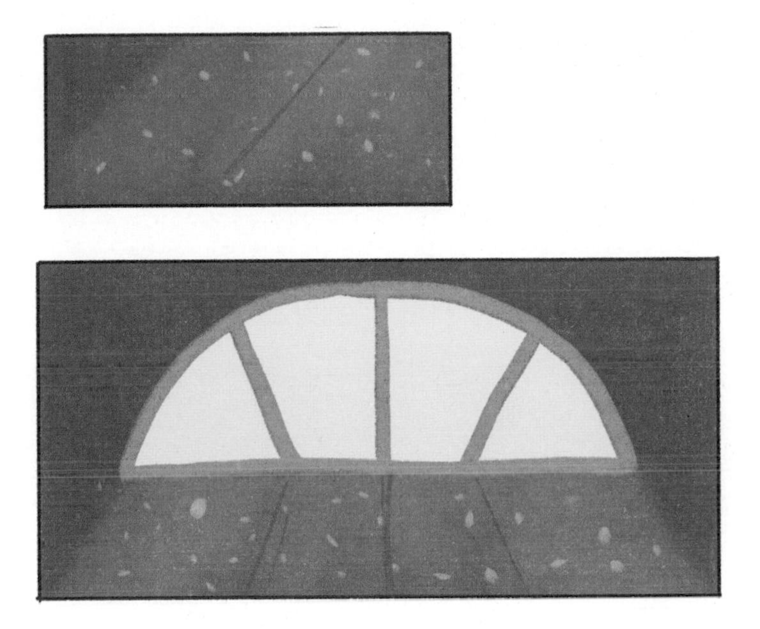

There must
be some way
I can find her.

History:

The Four Elements music

dachshund size

how do you pronounce . . .

Alexa Hudson 1977 obituary

Diana Rodriguez books

tap
The Oaksfield Daily

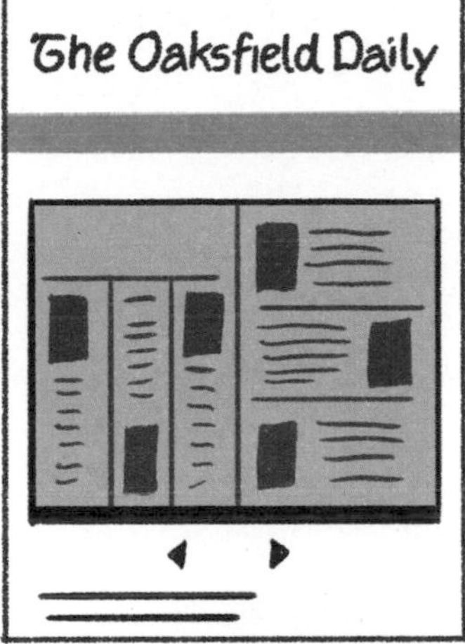
The Oaksfield Daily

Alexandra Hudson, d. 18 Sept, 1977
Fallen Oaks Cemetery
Buried at Fallen Oaks, huh?
Salem
03:30
How much time do I have?
Okay. Cool.
I got...
Salem
Three hours.
I can do this!
YEAH!

HI
I'm out on an errand. Will be back later—at 6? LORA
A R T Z
I'M READY!
LET'S GO!

Here I am.
04:01
I really hope you're here.

Gee,
I wonder what time it is...
OH. My. God.
WHAT.
05:33
Oh man, I'm gonna be so late. And I still haven't found Alexa's grave!
H'okay.
This graveyard is real deep.
If I run, maybe I can make it—
WHOAA!

CRACK
oof.

C'mon.
C'mon.
Oh no.
Don't tell me.
It's dead.
AH!
Ow...

groans
GAH!

How will I get out of here?

Nobody knows where I am.
I can't call anyone...
What happened to Alexa?
Is she...
Is she really gone?
BOOM
How long has it been?

URGH!
...
Am I gonna die here?
NO! No, no.
I won't die!
I'll find a way out somehow!
I won't be scared! It's okay. It's just—
breathes
It's just like being on an adventure.
Yeah! That's right!
I'm Lora Xi, world-famous explorer—
Currently inside the tomb...

. . . of an ancient storm god.
KRABOOM
My mission . . .
is to find my best friend, Alexa.

I'll escape this tomb.
And I'll find her.
C'mon, beast.
Show me what you got.

CRACK
Haha! Woo!
YES! Roar louder!
I'm not afraid of YOU!

gasps
You've come back.
It's been so long.

PPHREET

Oh.
What are -
-you doing?
WHOAA!

Oh wow.
Hello, w-where are we going?
Are you going to help me find Alexa?
snort

Thank you.
Okay.
Let's go.

Chapter 8:
The Magic Place

We're here.

Are you sure this is where you want to be dropped off?
Yes.
CAMP BUNLEY
PARKING
This hill has special meaning to me.

You've done so much for me today . . .
Thank you, Diana.
Especially for driving so slowly in the rain so I could keep up!
Ha ha!
It's all good!
I imagine it's not easy to sit in a car with an incorporeal body!
BBP BEEP BBBPQ BP
. . .
It was lovely to reconnect.
Reliving our childhood days . . .
I don't even mind how brief it was.
Me too.
I can't think of anyone better to spend my last day with.
chuckles
Best friends forever?
Best friends forever.

Oh, Alexa!
Will Lora be okay?
With you going?
Lora's at her first prom tonight. She will be with her friends . . .
If she's like any of the kids I used to play with—
She will be fine.

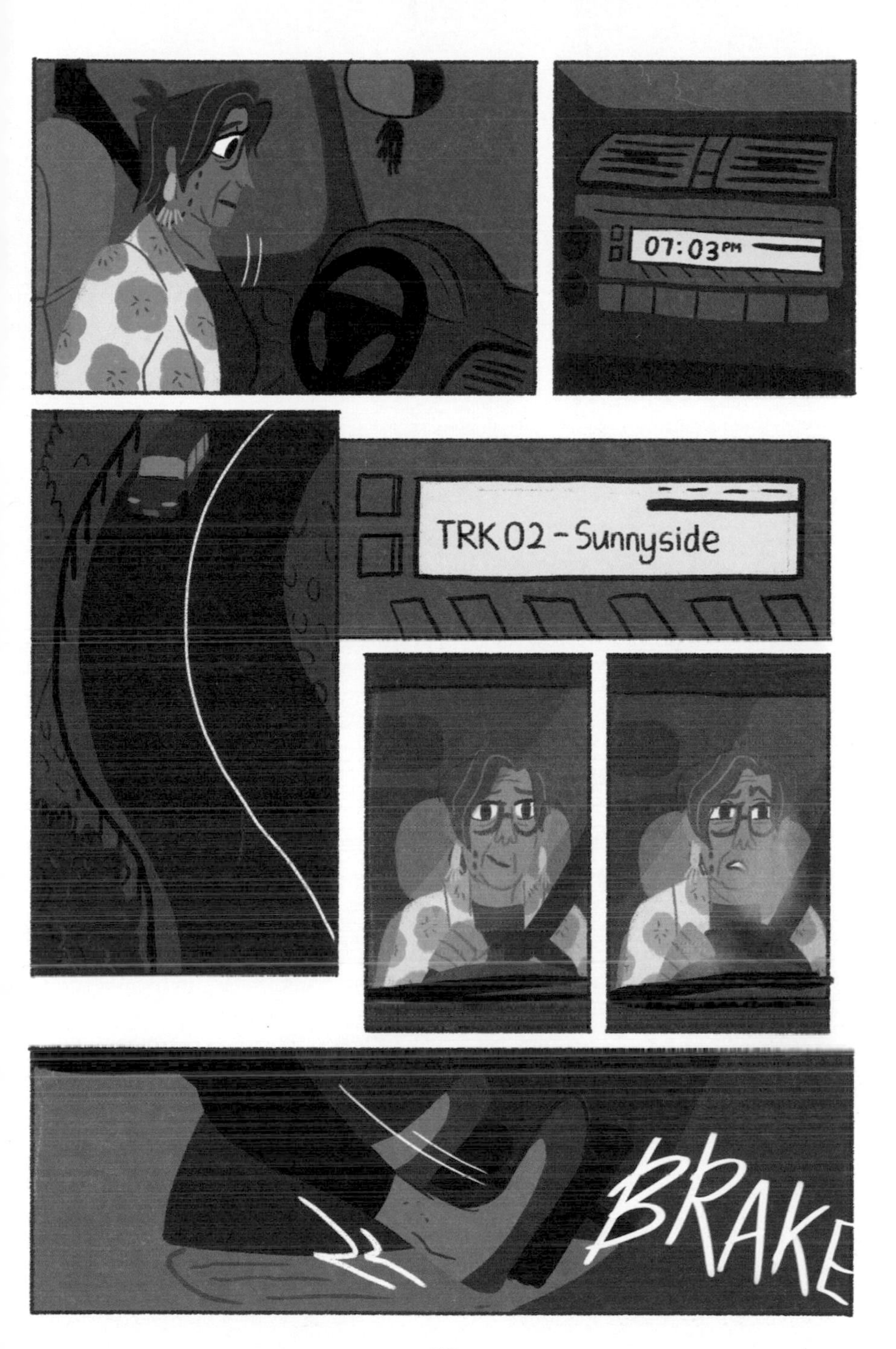
07:03PM
TRK 02 - Sunnyside
BRAKE

What's this?

¡Ay! ¡Dios mío!

The Fairies of Faring Forest!

WHOO!
I can't believe it!
My fairies!
They are real!

Alexa...
Alexa...
ALEXA!
Lora?
Wh-what are you doing here?

Alexa!
Where have you been?
Ohmygosh, I was so worried, I'm glad you'
AH!
OOF.
. . . Wait. Allie, are you okay?
You look... you look so faint.

How? Why? What's going on?

I remembered. That's why.

I know why I'm a ghost now.

Fifty years ago,
I died from an illness.

I barely got to live
my childhood.

So when I came back,
I forgot my old life
and became an
imaginary friend
to all the kids who lived
in the house after me.

Mikey.
Ella.
You.
I lived through your childhoods like they were mine.
And when each one of you grew up—
There was always the next one.
But I can't keep doing this forever.
Time doesn't care... sooner or later—
Everyone grows up.
They change.
They move on.

Even me.
NO!
Oof.
Do you — do you really have to go? Why can't you grow up with me?
I NEED to leave, Lora.
Besides —
You don't need me. You've already moved on with your own life.
You're grown up.
Grown up? Haha
What?
Wh-what made you think I was grown up?
Was it the makeup? The hair? The clothes? The internet jokes?
All that teen stuff?
Alexa!
I was only playing! I don't know what I'm doing at all!

The truth is...
I'm still scared.
I... I was only okay with getting older because —
I knew you'd always be here for me.
You remind me that I haven't yet lost who I am. That I still remember what magic is.
But now...
sobs

I–I'm so sorry—
For not being a better friend to you...
You mean so much to me.
You gave me a a happy childhood.
You were what made it magical.
sobs
Alexa. Please.
Don't leave.
I'm still not ready...
I don't... I don't know how to go on.
Lora.

You'll be okay. You won't ever lose that magic.
You know why?
Because I'm not that magic.
You are.
You created that magic as a kid.
You'll create that magic as a grown-up.
And you'll still do it even when you're old and gray.
There is nothing to be scared of—
When you have a whole life to look forward to.
sniff
And the best thing is, you won't be alone.
Really?
Really. I know.
This world is so big, and full of people who keep the magic in their lives.
When you see them —and you will— they will recognize you. Young or old.
And they will love you.

When I said you've grown up, what I meant was—
You've learned to live magically, all by yourself.
I don't want to be the one who holds you back.
And I need to move on and find my own life too.
Please, Lora, for the both of us—
Are you ready?
It's funny.
What is?
I planned to ask you to prom.
But then I had to goof up and sprain my ankle. And now I'm late.
Oh no!
It's okay.
I'm not upset about missing prom. There's always next year. Still...
It'd have been nice to go.

Y'know,
We can still have our own prom here.
Shall we dance?
But I can't touch you, and my ankle...
Hehe, silly.
We play pretend.
Now, c'mon—
Give me one last dance!
...
Sure. Let's.

Alexa. You still there...?
...
Oh.
Sorry. I didn't mean to...
I'll take my leave —
Wait.
Alexa already said goodbye.
She's finally moved on...
We both have.
OW!
What's wrong?

Are you hurt?
It's just a sprain.
Ouch.
Aunty.
You know Alexa...
Hm?
Who are you?
Ah.
I'm Diana.
I was Alexa's close friend in the old days.
And you, my dear...

You must be Lora.

epilogue

HAPPY BDAY

ALEXANDRA HUDSON
Hey, Manny!
My guy!
Be more careful, all right?

I almost got lost in this place once.
And do you know what happens to kids who get lost?
Nuh-uh.
They get caught by Bigfoot!
RAWR

Sigh.
Diana.
Do you miss her too?
ALEXANDRA HUDSON 1963–1977 Dearly beloved
Oh, yes, Lora.
Every day.
I keep thinking about what she told me before she left.
And I... I've no idea if I'm doing it right.
She said if I keep my magic, I'll find friends who get me.
Like you.
But I'm still scared.
How do I know if I'll be that adult she believed in?
What if I mess up?
I don't know, Diana.

It's confusing.
But that's what growing up is, no?
Not knowing, and being confused.
No adult has any idea what they're doing all the time, even me.
And that's not a bad thing.
You get to make your own choices, and see those choices through.
You'll lose yourself sometimes and then discover something new. You'll be remaking and developing who you are as you live and love.
Do you see it, Lora? This is magic by another name—
Freedom.
It's a blessing worth celebrating.
Speaking of celebrations...

Happy birthday.
HAPPY BDAY
bffs forever
Shall we make a toast?

To childhood.
ALEXANDRA HUDSON
And growing up.
And growing old.
And magic –
Whatever age we are.

ABCDEFG
NOPQRSTU
XYZ
12345

HAPPY BDAY
bffs forever
end

Acknowledgments

I acknowledge that this book was written and illustrated in Melbourne, Australia, and published in New York City, USA—on which the Wurundjeri people of the Kulin Nation and the Lenni Lenape people are the Traditional Custodians of their respective land. I pay my respect to their Elders both past, present, and emerging, and extend that respect to other First Nation people of Australia and Native Americans of North America.

I would like to express my gratitude to the team at Random House Graphic: Gina Gagliano, publisher powerhouse; Whitney Leopard, editor extraordinaire; Patrick Crotty, designer wizard; and Nicole Valdez, marketing magician. Thank you so much for believing in me as an author. It was a joy to work with you all.

As usual, I want to shower my agent Jen Linnan with a thousand and one biodegradable confetti, each spelling out "thanks!!" and "you're the best ♥♥♥"

I wish to send a shout-out to my friends and family who supported me during the making of *Séance Tea Party*, especially Nastasia, Alison, Kite, and Taylor for being my first readers.

Finally, thank you, reader, for picking up this book.

Reimena Yee is a strange and fancy illustrator, writer, and graphic novelist. Hailing from the dusty city of Kuala Lumpur, Malaysia, she originally studied STEM before pursuing her passion for the world and all of its histories and cultures.

She is the author-illustrator of the historical gothic fantasy *The Carpet Merchant of Konstantiniyya*, the first Malaysian graphic novel to be nominated for an Eisner Award. She is also the writer for the Makers Club series.

She has illustrated for multiple clients including Girls Make Games, the Adventure Time comics, Random House Children's Books, and Hasbro.

In addition, she is the cofounder of UNNAMED, a comics collective network created to build community and resources for visual-literary creators in Southeast Asia, through panels, workshops, and public outreach.

@reimenayee
@reimenayee
reimenayee.com • blog.reimenayee.com

Early character drawings and notes on Alexa and Lora. I drew these when I first told my publisher I wanted to make a book about them!

Lora Zi

• 12 years old
• quiet, lonely
• likes cryptids, weird phenomena, mythology.

The original artwork that inspired the story.
Drawn in 2016, done for fun!

After a few tries (at both drawing and writing), I ended up with a cast of three (and a half) main characters. These were their final designs.

The other characters came as the story developed.

Sunni was called a different name then.

My book designer, Patrick, and I tossed around some ideas for the cover. First, he gave me his sketches.

Then I drew my own sketches based on a few of Patrick's ideas I really liked.

We chose this one!

From sketch . . .

. . . to nearly finished!

Séance
Tea
party

Patrick made this very pretty text design for the title (better than mine, haha).

What you see on the front cover is a collaborative process with lots of talking and drawing involved.

Here's how I make comics.

I do an OUTLINE. I get the basic idea of how I want to tell a story and a character's journey, from start to end.

Then I spend a long time THINKING, aka DOING OTHER THINGS. During this time, the story will grow, change, get new ideas, lose old ones, and so on. I don't force my creativity, and I let my story ideas come to me whenever they want.

Once I have thought enough, I write a BIGGER OUTLINE. Then I get to writing the SCRIPT. This is what my script looks like.

I write using dialogue with minimal narrative direction, and little to no notes on the artwork. My focus when I write a script is on the story and characters. If both are strong, the art follows easily (for me anyway).

While she talks, she flips through the pages of the chapter: the White Lady, Bloody Mary, Will-o-Wisps, and seances...

> Lora: Hmm...feeling an idea coming...(snaps fingers) Let's hold a seance!

She turns to her toys.

> Lora: Not just a seance – a seance tea party! Whee-hee! (picks up her cat and bat plush) C'mon!

She brings up a tea set to the attic, as well as some birthday cake and a crystal ball. She makes an (inaccurate) ouija board and planchette out of cardboard and markers.

Arrange herself and her toys/fairies (guests) around a circle, she begins her seance, raising her toy wand.

> Lora: Bada-*zing*!

Nothing.

When my editor, Whitney, gives me the green light for the script, I move on to actually drawing the comic.

THUMBNAILS are little sketches of what I want a comic's page to look like. This is where I figure out where to place my characters, speech bubbles, and panels, and how all of those form an overall artistic composition. But they aren't the clearest. Compare these thumbnails with the final drawings. A big difference!

Afterward, I develop my thumbnails . . . sketches that look more like the final artwork. When I'm happy, I move on to . . .

THE ACTUAL DRAWING AND COLORING!

These are the two brushes I use in Photoshop.

Because of the art style of this book, I start by outlining the panel boxes, then FLATTING with various shades of black and gray to distinguish between characters, foreground objects, and backgrounds. Once I get the silhouettes done, I put in the real colors and details.

My Tools of the Trade
All the things I need to keep me writing, drawing & thinking.
scrap paper & notes
comics development moleskine
↳ concepts, thumbnails, ideas
ipad pro & apple pen (portable work device)
drawing apps:
• procreate
• clip studio
writing:
• goodnotes
DRINK OF THE DEAD
planner
(I love calendars and to-do lists.)
Work: 11am - 2pm
Break: 2pm - 6pm
Work: 7pm - 1 am
Social media:
twitter
tumblr
instagram
12 inch
PS
Photoshop
+Kyle Webster brushes
gmail
docs
libreoffice
notepad/textedit
Macbook Pro Mid 2012
Huion H610 Pro tablet
iphone 6+